For Katia and Tiziana.
S.P.
For my Mother and Father,
with love.
R.N.J.

First edition for the United States published 1992
by Barron's Educational Series, Inc.

Originally published as Chloe on the Climbing
Frame by J.M. Dent and Sons, Ltd, London,
1992.

Text copyright © Saviour Pirotta, 1992
Illustrations copyright © Rhian Nest-James,
1992

All inquiries should be addressed to:
Barron's Educational Series, Inc.
250 Wireless Boulevard
Hauppauge, New York 11788

International Standard Book No.
0–8120–6269–8 (hardcover)
0–8120–4829–6 (paperback)
Library of Congress Catalog Card No. 91–33194

**Library of Congress
Cataloging-in-Publication Data**

Pirotta, Saviour.
Chloe on the jungle gym/Saviour Pirotta;
illustrated by Rhian Nest-James.
p.   cm.
Summary: Chloe meets a brown bear at the
top of the park jungle gym and flies around the
world with him to meet other bear friends in
China, the Arctic, and the American West.
ISBN 0–8120–6269–8 (hard).
ISBN 0–8120–4829–6 (pbk)
[1. Bears—Fiction.] I. James, Rhian Nest, 1962–, ill.
II. Title.   91–33194
PZ7. P6425Ch 1992   CIP
[E]—dc20   AC

PRINTED IN ITALY
2345 0987654321

Chloe
on the
JUNGLE
GYM

Saviour Pirotta

Illustrated by

Rhian Nest-James

Right at the end of Seashell Street there is a park. It is full of trees and grass, and at the back there is a small playground.

Chloe and her father often go there to play. Sometimes they build castles in the sandpile and at other times they play on the swings.

Once, when Dad fell asleep on the grass,
Chloe climbed up the jungle gym.

It was a long way to the top. Chloe
brushed past the trees. She climbed through
the clouds. At last she reached a little hut
with a bright yellow door and a gray,
puffing chimney.

"I never knew this jungle gym was so high," Chloe said out loud.

"Well, it is," said a voice from inside the hut.

The yellow door opened and a little brown bear came out.

"Hello," he said. "Did you see my bobble hat on your way up?"

"I'm afraid I didn't," Chloe replied.

Brown Bear looked worried.

"Oh, dear," he said, "I must have left it at one of my cousin's."

He popped back indoors and returned with a suitcase.

"Come on," he said. "Let's go."

"Yes, let's," Chloe said.

Brown Bear opened the suitcase and took out a green carpet with igloos and icebergs around the border.

"Hop aboard," he said to Chloe.

Chloe sat behind the bear and held on to his furry waist.

"Yip Yop Yay," said Brown Bear.

The carpet leaped off the jungle gym. Chloe felt the wind rush through her hair.

"Right, left, right," Brown Bear shouted.

The carpet traveled over the town, soared over the sea, and turned toward the frozen North. Chloe began to feel cold.

Soon they landed on an iceberg and Brown Bear knocked on a door.

"Come in," someone called.

Chloe and Brown Bear crept into the igloo.

"This is my cousin Polar," said Brown Bear. "And this is his friend Sofie."

Sofie made them a cup of hot tea and Polar gave them something to eat.

"Did I leave my bobble hat in here yesterday?" asked Brown Bear.

"No," said Polar and Sofie. "Maybe it's outside."

Sofie, Polar and Chloe built a snowbear and a snowgirl while Brown Bear searched in the snow. He asked the puffins and the seals, but no one had seen his hat.

"I must have left it at Cousin Panda's," Brown Bear said. "Come on, Chloe, let's go!"

He opened his suitcase and pulled out a bamboo mat with kites and lanterns around the border.

"Yip Yop Yay," he said.
    The mat raced over rivers and leaped over lakes. It headed for the East. Chloe began to feel warm.

Brown Bear stopped the mat in the shade of some bamboo near a house.

"Hello," he called.

"Hello," replied two voices from inside.

Brown Bear opened the door. "This is my cousin Panda and my friend Wu."

"Hello, Chloe," said Wu and Panda. "Would you like some noodles?"

While Chloe ate from a china bowl, Brown Bear went off to find his hat. He looked all over the house but couldn't find it.

Chloe finished her noodles and helped Wu and Panda make a kite.
It was hard work trying to fly it, so Chloe took off her jacket and
laid it on the ground. Brown Bear came back empty-handed.

"I might have left it at cousin Grizzly's," he said. "Come on,
Chloe, let's go!"

He opened his suitcase and took out a brightly colored mat with
wigwams and campfires around the border.

"Yip Yop Yay," he said.
The mat shot into the sky
and flew over forests to the
mountains in the West.
Chloe could smell pine
needles and summer corn.

Brown Bear landed the mat next to a wigwam. "Hello," called a boy and a big bear peeping out of the tent.

"This is my cousin Grizzly," Brown Bear said. "And this is my friend Little Feather."

Then he went off to look for his hat.

Little Feather and Grizzly showed Chloe how to fish in the stream. Chloe took off her shoes and socks and waded in the water. While the fish was cooking, Chloe put her shoes back on again.

Brown Bear came back looking very pleased. "I've found my hat," he cried. "I'd left it near a honeycomb."

Little Feather and Grizzly gave him some roasted corn. Chloe ate some fish.

Then it was time to fly back to the jungle gym. Brown Bear looked in the suitcase and pulled out a mat with clouds and jungle gyms around the border.

"Yip Yop Yay," he said and the mat flew back across China, took a shortcut over the North Pole, and then flew south to Seashell Street.

"Thanks for coming with me," Brown Bear said.

"Thanks for taking me," said Chloe.

She kissed Brown Bear goodbye and hurried down the jungle gym.

"Goodness me," said Dad who had just awakened. "Look at the time."

He took Chloe's hand and they went home.

"Where's your coat?" Mom asked. "And where are your socks and your scarf?"

"Oh, dear," Chloe cried. "I left my coat in China, my socks out West, and my scarf in the Arctic."

Dad looked rather puzzled.

"A likely story," Mom said.

A week later there were three packages in the mail for Chloe.
   One had come all the way from the Arctic, one from China, and one from out West.
   "I wonder what's inside them." Mom said.
   Chloe just smiled.
   "Why don't you open them and see?" she said.